The Attic Mice

THE
ATTIC MICE

Ethel Pochocki

Pictures by
DAVID CATROW

Henry Holt and Company ◆ *New York*

Published by Henry Holt and Company, Inc.,
115 West 18th Street, New York, New York 10011.
Published in Canada by Fitzhenry & Whiteside Limited,
195 Allstate Parkway, Markham, Ontario L3R 4T8.

Library of Congress Cataloging-in-Publication Data
Pochocki, Ethel.
The attic mice / Ethel Pochocki ; illustrated by David Catrow.
Summary: Recounts the adventures of a family of mice as they go
shopping in the humans' kitchen, discover useful items in the attic,
and celebrate Christmas.
ISBN 0-8050-1298-2
[1. Mice—Fiction.] I. Catrow, David, ill. II. Title.
PZ7.P7495At 1990
[Fic]—dc20   90-32064

Henry Holt books are available at special discounts
for bulk purchases for sales promotions, premiums,
fund-raising, or educational use. Special editions
or book excerpts can also be created to specification.

First Edition

Printed in the United States of America
on acid-free paper. ♾

1 3 5 7 9 10 8 6 4 2

To Arnold and Gertrude with love
                                              —E.P.

To Deborah, for all your
love and support
                              —D.C.

Go, little Book; from this my solitude,
    I cast thee on the waters:—go thy ways!
And if, as I believe, thy vein be good,
    The World will find thee, after many days.
Be it with thee according to thy worth:—
Go, little Book! in faith I send thee forth

—*Robert Southey*

Contents

1 ◆ LITTLE-GOOD-FOR-NOTHING 1

2 ◆ THE ATTIC MICE 17

3 ◆ OMELETTA'S DOWNSTAIRS ADVENTURE 33

4 ◆ CHESTER'S RARE AFFLICTION 51

5 ◆ A PRIVATE PLACE FOR PRIM 72

6 ◆ THE ATTIC CRÈCHE 90

7 ◆ EPILOGUE 108

The Attic Mice

·1·

Little-Good-for-Nothing

here was once a small chestnut* who had nothing to do but swing from the limb of his tree. He did not think about getting good marks at school or eating boiled turnips or keeping his white socks clean. He thought about nothing because all he knew was nothing.

He was wrapped in darkness, snug in the pocket of the hard green burr. He didn't know about the color green—that it was the color of grass and limes and emeralds—or about the colors of peaches or robins' eggs. He didn't know about woodpeckers or rabbits or the sparkle of sun on a spiderweb.

---

*This chapter is really the story of a chestnut. But because it was through the chestnut I met the attic mice, I felt it deserved a place in their book.

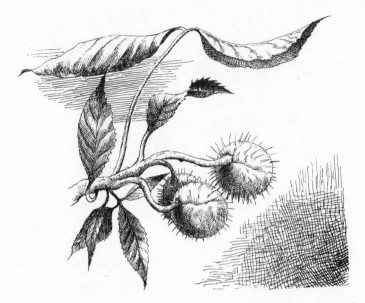

The little horse chestnut knew only the joy of bouncing with the wind, whichever way it might blow. He danced along with its song, which sometimes whined frail and high and sometimes shrieked in fury. Sometimes, when the wind was gentle and teasing, he just lay still and listened to the world outside his shell.

He heard the spring song of frogs, and crickets fiddling on a September eve. He heard the careful step of the fox and the quick trot of the cat running from him. He heard the bark of hungry hounds and the laughter of humans.

All these sounds he heard but could not name. Only when his friend the chipmunk sat beside him on the limb and told him of the wind and the fox and the crickets did the little horse chestnut try to imagine their shapes and colors. But he did not do very well, for how could he imagine the sweep of a fox's golden tail or a frog catching flies with his tongue, when all he knew was *nothing*?

One autumn day a wind came out of the north, grey and gruff and looking for mischief. He joined another bully from the west who felt the same way. Together they howled around the chestnut tree and rattled and throttled its branches, until it bowed and let the winds have their way.

The fat chestnuts from the top of the tree fell first and pelted the ground like a shower of marbles. The little horse chestnut was shaken and tossed harder than ever before. Suddenly he heard a *snap* and felt himself falling, falling, over and over. He landed with such a hard thud, his green burr cracked open right down the middle.

At once the world he had never known burst open before him, and the blinding blur of colors dazzled him. Never could he have imagined such beauty! The sun warmed him, and he saw for the first time his satiny brown skin. He met his friend the chipmunk, who rushed to tell him the names of everything in sight. She chattered faster and faster in the excitement of sharing her knowledge.

For days he listened to the chipmunk and lay among the other chestnuts, watching them pop forth from their burrs, now dried crisp and prickly in the sun. Then, early one morning, a snowflake fell silent and unnoticed onto a red maple leaf near him on the ground. Then another, and another, and another fell and joined it, until soon all the leaves were frosted with snow.

A whisper of November wind shivered the leaves yet clinging to the mother chestnut tree. It rustled through the black, bare limbs, reminding, "It's time. . . . It's time. . . ."

The tree understood. Every year with the first flurry of snow, it happened. The humans came with

baskets and bags and gathered up the chestnuts. They dug under the leaves and dead grass and gnarled tree roots, and found every chestnut that had fallen. The humans groaned with the weight of baskets heaped high and bags bowing their backs. When they left, only cracked brown burrs remained.

The humans who came this day were a mother and her children. What a good year this is, thought the mother. I've never seen such beauties. They should bring a good price.

She held a chestnut in her hand, enjoying its soft, warm comfort. The brown was the color of her mother's hair when she was young. She wished the chestnuts could be eaten. How delicious a pan of roasted, buttery chestnuts would taste on this winter's night!

But she knew their only purpose was to give beauty. The family would sell them to the wreath maker, and he would use them to decorate the wreaths he sold at market. It was a gathering time that made everyone happy. Even the chestnuts, clustered on the sweet balsam boughs, knew their moment of pride.

This year the mother made sure no nut went unnoticed. She and her children each grabbed a bag or took hold of a basket handle and began the walk home. The snowflakes began to tumble in earnest. "Hurry," she called to her youngest. "Don't dawdle!"

The little boy had stopped, for at the base of the tree he spied one very small chestnut everyone had overlooked.

"I've found one," he called out, "and he's just right for me!"

"Nothing doing," said his mother. "Every one goes into the basket. Even little-good-for-nothing here. Heavens, he's tiny—he's not big enough to make a coat button, let alone be on a Christmas wreath. Still, every bit helps. Into the basket with you!"

So that's my name, thought the horse chestnut. Little-Good-for-Nothing. I hope that's not right. I must be good for *something*. Of course I am. I'll be on a Christmas wreath too. I know I will.

He didn't know what a Christmas wreath was, but he was certain it was a special honor to be on one.

When the family reached home, they carried their sacks and baskets into the kitchen, by the wood stove. Nora, the ringleader of the kittens, jumped immediately onto the heap of chestnuts in one basket, slipping, sliding, and clutching onto them for dear life. Little-Good-for-Nothing, who had been perched on top, bumped down over the others and rolled to the floor.

Max, the old tomcat, woke from his pillow on the rocker and watched Nora through half-open eyes. Max did not like the kittens. They were a bother, always underfoot, in the way, pests. They ate the food in his special dish. They climbed over him when he slept, pounced on his tail, mewed in his ear or chewed on it when they dared, until he gave a long, low, threatening growl and they fled.

Then he would close his eyes and return to his dreams, remembering his days of youth and his strength as a mighty hunter. On this day, just as he was about to overcome the largest, meanest mouse known to man or cat, he was startled awake by the sound of the chestnuts scattering the floor.

His mind and one good eye still foggy with sleep, he saw Little-Good-for-Nothing skitter across his view, and he believed him to be the vicious enemy of his dream. He roused himself quickly. He must be alert, at the ready to rid his world of this intruder. A mouse in his kitchen? Impossible!

He slid off the rocker with as much stealth as his heavy stomach would allow and picked his way across the wooden floor. He hunched low, twitched his whiskers, quivered his charged-up tail, and then—*sprang!* He landed square upon the little chestnut and began to bat it about, this way and that, with his paw.

Nora, always ready for a good squabble, jumped in front of him, picked up Little-Good-for-Nothing in her mouth, and carried him to her hideaway of treasures under the living-room couch.

Max ignored the young upstart and sauntered back to the rocker with the grace of a victor. "So much for that mouse," he yawned. He jumped up to his pillow, still warm from his interrupted nap, and returned to a world awaiting his conquest.

Little-Good-for-Nothing lay in his home under the couch right through Thanksgiving and Christmas and Groundhog Day and Valentine's Day. He was quite alone except for a piece of tinsel, a spool of green thread, and a very old and dried apple core.

One morning in March the mother decided it was

time for spring cleaning. The family took down the storm windows and grimy curtains and swept cobwebs from the ceiling and washed the good china with the gold rims. Then they moved the furniture and rolled up the rugs.

It was then that the young boy found Little-Good-for-Nothing again. He was still smooth and shiny, and the boy picked him up quickly so he would not have to give up his treasure again. He didn't know what he would do with him, so he just held him and dreamed of all the wonderful things he *could* do.

He might juggle him or play marbles with him or put a hole through him and wear him around his neck and pretend to be a brave of a lost Indian tribe, or he might just throw him into the stove to hear him pop. But then he would lose him forever. So the boy kept him in his jacket pocket as a magic amulet, which when rubbed in the light of the quarter moon would turn the boy into a flying white horse that could travel the world before the sun rose.

All the while the chestnut nestled deep in the boy's pocket, the sun warmed the earth and hinted of spring. Soon the boy could run about without boots or sweater. His mother packed the mittens and scarves and jackets away in the attic, emptying the pockets of old cough drops stuck with fuzz, pencil stubs, rubber bands, and gum wrappers. Somehow she missed Little-Good-for-Nothing, hidden deep down among some cookie crumbs.

However it came to be, the horse chestnut found himself in the attic, packed snugly away with the winter clothes. He was warm and safe in the dark, just as he had been before he fell to earth, but now he was no longer contented. Now he knew what he was missing, and he wanted to be back in the world, even if it could be dangerous.

He feared it was lost to him forever. There seemed no way of rescue, and he passed the time sadly sorting through his memories, savoring them as one might a cup of hot chocolate on a bitter-cold day. He wondered if he would ever see the sun again, or the boy, or even old Max.

The little chestnut might have gone on in this dreary way forever had he not been found by the attic mice and brought home to live with them.

· 2 ·

The Attic Mice

The attic mice were a family of five. Arnold, the father, had been a librarian in the stacks at the University, and Gertrude, the mother, had been a pantry mouse in the home of the Dean. They were introduced at a church social given by the chapel mice, and from the moment their eyes met, they knew they were meant to marry.

They first set up house in a stable, but Gertrude was terrified of being trampled by the horses, so they moved to the wine cellar of a nearby inn. Arnold began to get tipsy from smelling the corks, and Gertrude, who would drink only home-brewed birch beer, felt it wise not to stay. When they heard through friends of the vacant farmhouse in the attic, they investigated, liked it, and settled down to raise their family there.

Their three children were, in their parents' eyes, remarkably unique. Primrose, the oldest, always called Prim because she was very serious and proper, had what Gertrude called "an inclination for the arts." Chester, the second child, was named for Arnold's father, who was a pioneer in mouse photography. Omeletta, who was born unexpectedly in an egg carton, was a tomboy and a tease and boasted that anything Chester could do, she could do better—and she usually could.

The mice lived comfortably in the old doll farm-house, which sat in the center of a blue-checkered linoleum yard. It was not really a yard, but Gertrude, being practical, said it was just as well, since children would only ruin a lawn. In her heart, though, she did wish they had a bit of land to grow corn. To the left of the house, a red wooden silo stood guard, and behind that was a barn with a hayloft and real doors that opened to let out the farm animals and tractor.

The buildings were sturdy but in need of paint. They had been outgrown by the human children and stored in the attic for years before the mice moved in. Arnold and Gertrude (especially Gertrude) had dreamed of a different kind of home—a grand Victorian dollhouse, perhaps, with wicker rockers on a wraparound porch, a trellis with climbing roses in front. A library, of course, and a music room, and a balcony or two. Gertrude had always wanted her own balcony.

But they were cheerful, adaptable mice who believed in making the most of what they had. Gertrude made a comfortable home. She hung prisms of beach glass in the windows, and in summer put bowls of nasturtiums on a lace cloth on the dining-room table. In winter she used a silver thimble (given at marriage by her mother) filled with dried baby's breath instead.

On Sunday afternoons the mice went adventuring. This was the day they explored whatever new boxes had come up to the attic during the week. The children could hardly wait to rummage. Always a treat awaited them, bits of this and that which could bring pleasure only to a mouse family.

On this Sunday they ate their meal of beach-pea soup and corn muffins with plum jam and cleaned up quickly without even a hint of quarreling. Then they were on their way—Chester in the lead, Omeletta on his heels, then Arnold smoking his pipe, and finally Gertrude, holding tight to Prim.

When they reached the new box, each chose a different spot to chew, pry, and tug, until they at last loosened the top enough to crawl in one at a time.

All of them had special dreams. Prim hoped for a crumpled tissue, colored if possible, to make a

bouquet of paper roses, or an acorn she could use for a top. Omeletta wished for a shoelace she could use as a jump rope, or a rubber band, which would make a perfect slingshot against Chester.

Arnold would have been happy to find a burnt matchstick to use as a log for the fire, or an old theater-ticket stub, so he might know what was happening in the outside world (sometimes he did miss his carefree bachelor days in the library). Gertrude would be satisfied with a few sunflower seeds for her ginger cookies, or a frilly candy wrapper to use as a candy dish.

Chester would have settled for anything. He was bored with life. He didn't want to read and he didn't want to color or shelve books for his father or play Anagrams with the family. All he wanted to do was sit by the window and write in his journal about how bored he was.

So it was by happy chance that Chester was the one to find Little-Good-for-Nothing. "Look!" he cried, as he held up the tiny chestnut for all to see. "Look what I've found, and he's mine, all mine!"

"Just a moment, Chester," said his father, quietly excited, but prudent. "I'd like to have a look at that." Everyone remembered the time Chester had brought home a camphor mothball and told Omeletta it was a giant sugar mint and dared her to eat it. That had been a close call. Ever since, they had been wary when Chester found something.

"Why, it's a lovely horse chestnut," Gertrude exclaimed.

"Please let me have it, Papa! I want it, it's just right for a soccer ball. Please, please!" Chester screwed up his face so hard, a tear almost formed on his cheek. Then, just as he had feared, the girls began their clamor.

Omeletta tried to grab Little-Good-for-Nothing from him. "It's not fair. It's not just for you, you've got to share. Give it here—I need it for a hockey puck. You'd better share or I'll hit you hard. Mother, tell him to share!"

Then Prim cleared her throat and dropped her words like tiny bits of ice. "Mother, *I* think the chestnut would be perfect for me to use as a door-stop in my bedroom. I would paint flowers on it. I don't think anything so nice should be kicked around."

"Oh, Miss Prissy Prim," snickered Omeletta, "you *never* want to do anything that's fun, and you don't want anyone else to, either. You're such a royal pain!"

"Now, children," said Arnold firmly, "you must stop this bickering. You all have good uses for the chestnut, but don't you think your mother and I should share it also? I don't like to think you are selfish children."

Chester, Omeletta, and Prim looked down at the floor in silence.

"Now," continued Arnold, "I think our chestnut would make a very nice paperweight for my papers, so they won't fly all over the den when the door's opened."

"And," added Gertrude, "I would like it as a footstool at night when I'm mending clothes."

Little-Good-for-Nothing felt quite proud. All the mice wanted him for themselves! He would have been happy to please any one of them.

Prim was given the honor of bearing him home. Then she held him in her lap in the rocker while Gertrude put up the kettle for sassafras tea.

Over their cups of tea and caraway-seed cookies, Arnold and Gertrude decided that Little-Good-for-Nothing would go first to Omeletta and Chester together, since they had the least amount of patience. Prim sniffed that it wasn't fair, but said no more than that.

With loud whoops of joy and clashing of wood, Chester and Omeletta began to play field hockey. They made such a racket, they woke the humans in the rooms below. Annoyed at having his sleep disturbed, the human father opened the attic door for Max to go up and put an end to those varmints.

When Omeletta and Chester heard the human father send Max into the attic, they grabbed the chestnut and fled to the safety of the farmhouse, where the others were playing a lively game of Authors.

"Max is coming—hurry, bolt the door!" cried Chester. All the mice went into position, as they had been trained. They tried not to squeak, sneeze, cough, or breathe loudly. Max was old and half blind, but he was the enemy still and they must be on guard.

For what seemed a long time (actually only six

minutes, according to Arnold's pocket watch), they crouched low in the darkened parlor of the farmhouse, their eyes barely at the level of the windowsills, waiting to hear the soft padding of cat feet going back downstairs. But there was nothing. No meow, no scratch, no flick of a whisker, no crash of boxes—what was he doing?

Gertrude was afraid the children's breathing might ruffle the curtains and attract attention. Then the attic ceiling light flashed on and lit up the farmhouse.

"On the floor, everyone!" whispered Arnold, ever courageous in time of crisis. "Flatten, and not a sound!"

"Max?" called the human father. "Max? Where are you? Come down, you old grouch. I'm not going to wait all night. Now hurry up." Max came out from under the eaves and lurched down the stairs.

Gertrude lit the oil lamps, calmed the children, and got them ready for bed. The mice had weathered the danger; now they were back, snug and secure, to the way things had been. Just when it seemed the children were dropping off, Omeletta said, "I wish Max had swallowed a mothball," and set them all to laughing.

Prim, wanting to have the last word, said sleepily, "Don't forget, *I* get the chestnut tomorrow."

And so she did. First she painted pansies on Little-Good-for-Nothing and used him as her door-stop. Then, when no one was looking, she placed the chestnut on her head and practiced walking gracefully, so she would not slump. She imagined herself as Princess Primrose and felt she had been born to it.

Then Arnold used him to hold down his papers.

The manuscript (he was writing a book on mouse fairy-legends) grew higher and higher, but the little chestnut sat firmly atop the pile, keeping it in order.

And in the evening, when the family gathered in the living room by the fire to read, Gertrude put a small, fat pine-needle pillow on the chestnut and rested her feet upon him.

Little-Good-for-Nothing had indeed become part of the family, part of their daily life and special celebrations. His greatest moment of pride was at Christmas, when Prim made a wreath of fir tips that Arnold had brought from the woods, and put the little chestnut right smack in the middle of it. She hung it on the farmhouse door with a piece of red gingham ribbon.

The chestnut's long-ago dream of being handsome enough to grace a wreath had come true.

·3·

Omeletta's Downstairs Adventure

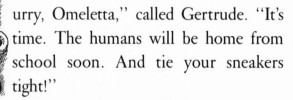

Hurry, Omeletta," called Gertrude. "It's time. The humans will be home from school soon. And tie your sneakers tight!"

Gertrude went over her shopping list again. She closed her eyes and thought very intently of anything she might have missed. Ah, yes, caraway seeds. She wrote it carefully at the bottom of the paper and then read the list aloud to herself in a singsong voice, as if it were a poem. Indeed, she thought, a well-crafted shopping list could be very satisfying, and she continued to recite:

curly pretzels
dried currants
peanuts for peanut
butter
peanuts for eating
wax

green beans
matches
bitter orange marm.
peppermint toothpaste
arrowroot biscuits
Limburger cheese
baby aspirin
brown rice
Slippery Elm cough
drops
paprika
paper clips
1 cinnamon stick
pinto beans or dried
peas or both
horseradish mustard
ginger ale
raisins
caraway seeds

Gertrude knew she would not find everything on
her list, but she was flexible and would be content
with whatever she found in the Downstairs pantry.

Still, she felt more efficient if she had a list.

Usually she and Arnold made the venture in the middle of the night, when Max and the humans were in a deep sleep, but today Gertrude and Omeletta would make a daytime foray. Arnold had taken Prim and Chester on a mushroom-hunting expedition, so he could teach them which were safe to eat.

"Well, my dear," he had said as he kissed Gertrude good-bye, "wish us luck. Perhaps we shall find a truffle."

"Ugh!" said Prim, who had read about truffles in her French book. "Mushrooms are nasty enough, but ugly old mushrooms you have to dig for—ugh! I'll never eat one."

"My dear, a truffle is no trifle," smiled her father, pleased with his wordplay. "Once you are older, you will appreciate what a delicacy it is."

"*Blah*," shuddered Prim. "If I live to be a hundred and ninety-four, I'll never eat a truffle."

"Never mind, you two," said Gertrude, anxious for them to get going. "Just a nice chanterelle will do, dear. Now, off with you, and don't get your feet

wet!'' And she hustled them out the door, Chester
and Arnold leading the way, and Prim, sucking on
a lemon drop, skipping a small distance behind
them.

"Now, Omeletta, are we ready?'' Gertrude asked
briskly. There was no more time to dillydally. The
mistress had gone out—where, Gertrude did not
know. Perhaps shopping. Taking care of her loved
ones. The thought of the human mother shopping
for food for her family warmed Gertrude's heart.
How similar we are, she mused. Too bad the human
mother doesn't feel the same way about us.

"All set!" said Omeletta, shivering with excitement. She couldn't believe that *she* was going Downstairs, that *she* would get to see the bins and cupboards and baskets she had heard her parents talk about.

Lightheartedly mother and daughter hurried down the attic stairs, their soft feet making no sound. Max should be outside napping in the sun, but just in case—they would take no chances.

They left the attic door ajar for their return. Gertrude put down the picnic basket filled with tape and string and thimble and scissors and rested for a moment before continuing down the winding back-kitchen stairs.

"Oh, what fun!" squealed Omeletta, and before her mother could stop her, she scrambled up the banister, tucked her skirt and apron under her, and whisked swiftly down the polished railing, landing happily in a wash basket of freshly folded towels.

"Omeletta, don't you ever do that again!" gasped Gertrude. "You nearly scared me out of my wits. And we need all the wits we can get on this trip, so shape up!"

They ran across the wooden kitchen floor into the pantry. Omeletta thought this must be what Mouse Heaven was like. Bushels of turnips and carrots and apples and green tomatoes, and their good smells blending together; bins of dry beans and rice and tea bags; cans of cloves and nutmeg and sassafras tea; jars of green pickles and gold peaches and pink applesauce lining the shelves. Omeletta was surprised that humans put away food in jars too.

When she tired of helping her mother stuff cranberries and celery seed and smoked almonds and birthday candles into the basket, she ran over to Max's rocker and jumped up into its almost threadbare cushion. She circled it and, with her feet, tore tiny tufts of thread from its raggedy face.

"This'll throw Max into a tizzy," she laughed. "He'll *smell* mouse, but he won't *find* mouse!"

Gertrude, busy with her foraging, smiled. Children could be such a tease.

Suddenly they heard the sound of soft humming, heels clicking on the linoleum floor, and bags being emptied onto the table. Omeletta fled the rocker and, with her mother, dove deep into a nearby bin of lentils. They didn't dare move, lest they cause an avalanche. The mistress kept humming as she put away cans of soup and bunches of broccoli and celery. Then she got out a bowl of sugar and the vanilla and poured a small carton of cream into a shiny steel bowl.

"There now, we'll have whipped cream to go with our blueberry cake tonight. But first," the mistress continued, talking to herself, "I've *got* to get into my comfortable old clothes," and she left the kitchen, her heels clicking all the way upstairs.

"Did you hear that?" whispered Gertrude to Omeletta. "Did you *see* that? Cream! Oh, what I wouldn't give for whipped cream on our pumpkin tarts tonight!"

"Cream," murmured Omeletta. "I can taste it right now. Oatmeal and cream, apple crisp and cream, strawberries and cream, just plain cream and cream! Ohhhh. . . ." she groaned, her eyes closed.

"We've got to get some," decided Gertrude. "We're so close—opportunity is knocking. Let's get out of these lentils—carefully now, no noise. The sun is going down and Max will be in—hurry!"

Slowly they shook themselves free of lentils, and quietly, single file, they ran up and over the drawers of rolling pins, silverware, and dish towels, up to the counter where the bowl of cream sat waiting to be whipped.

"Now, here's the plan," said Gertrude. "Climb up onto the edge of the bowl and lower this thimble into it, and then hand it back to me. I have a cover for it. Be very careful, keep your balance, and don't fall in. We have no time for mistakes."

"Don't worry, I can do it." Omeletta felt proud that she was the one helping her mother. It could have been Prim, or, worse, Chester.

The good rich smell of the cream made her whiskers twitch with eagerness. She lowered the thimble with care, her hind feet grasping the rim of the bowl tightly. As she waited for the thimble to fill, she heard the mistress's feet running lightly down the stairs and the humming coming closer.

"Oh dear," cried Gertrude.
"Never mind, Omeletta—
don't freeze! I'm coming up to get you!"

Before Omeletta could say "No!" Gertrude was
on the rim, and the bowl, heavy under their weight,
toppled. The cream splashed over the countertop,
covering Gertrude and Omeletta, then dribbled
down in several streams to the floor.

The mice screamed in panic and, momentarily

blinded by the cream, ran madly in all directions. Gertrude stumbled and fell into the bowl of sugar and was followed by Omeletta, who jumped in after her mother. They opened their eyes, rubbed them dry, and screamed again when they saw each other.

"Omeletta?" squeaked Gertrude.

"Mother?" squeaked Omeletta in return.

"You look like a ghost!" said Gertrude.

"You too!" said Omeletta.

The steps came closer and then stopped at the sight of the spilled cream.

"What on earth—"

"Let's get out of here," whispered Gertrude, grabbing the heavy picnic basket.

The two sugar-coated mice made the journey from countertop to floor in no time.

"The thimble! We forgot the thimble," remembered Omeletta.

"Forget the thimble—let's *go!*" said Gertrude.

While the mistress angrily wiped up cream from the counter, they ran along the woodwork of the kitchen, which was also white and so hid them somewhat. Once into the hallway, they dashed up the back stairs and attic stairs as fast as they could. They looked like two speeding blobs of cotton.

When they reached the barnyard, Omeletta flopped down and gasped for breath. "Mother, *please* don't ask me to go shopping again—or at least not

until I'm an old lady and have lived most of my life!"

"Look at us," said Gertrude. "Two white mice, all creamy and sticky with sugar. Good enough to eat!" And she reached over and tweaked a few drops from Omeletta's whiskers. "Mmm, delicious!"

Not to be outdone, Omeletta jumped up and licked the cream from one, then both, of her mother's ears, until the gray fur showed through. "How strange—a white mouse with gray ears!" And they started laughing all over again.

"What if your father saw us!"

"Prim would say, 'Ugh! You look worse than truffles!' "

"Oh well." Gertrude wiped away her tears. "We did get some necessary groceries. You know, I think we deserve a reward. Something for the nerves. I'll run the water for a hot tub and put some lavender flowers in it, and we'll just soak in our milk bath and read the paper and loll around, the way ladies do in the afternoon before tea. It does wonders for the complexion. Your grandmother never had a wrinkle, even when she died. Of course, she died young—fell into an open pickle barrel. But she still had a lovely complexion. And then I shall make a pot of lentil soup with a bay leaf and peppercorns and carrot dumplings. Perhaps roast truffle, too, if your father has good luck."

By suppertime the weary hunters had arrived home with wet feet, red ears, and a large brown bag of something. Chester was sniffling and had bleary eyes. "I'm sorry, my dear," Arnold said with a slight smile. "No mushrooms. Someone got there before us. But Chester and I found some acorns for roasting, and one whole ear of strawberry popcorn still on the stalk. So we stripped it right then and there."

"No wonder your pockets are bulging. What a wonderful treat," said Gertrude graciously. Men did need to feel appreciated. "I'm sure we'll enjoy popcorn even more than a truffle. Chester, whatever happened to your clothes? You're a mess."

"Now, don't be too hard on the boy, Gertrude,"

said Arnold. "He was trying to bring you a surprise, risked life and limb climbing up a monstrous sunflower head. He was digging the seeds out one by one and throwing them down to me, when a crow flew overhead and squawked at him, in that annoying way they have. He was so unnerved, he fell to the ground and landed in a rotten tomato. Well, to add insult to injury, you know how he *hates* tomatoes—"

"Poor boy," said Gertrude, hugging her tomato-splattered son. "You are so thoughtful."

She turned to her eldest daughter. "And what about you, Prim? What did you find?"

"Well," said Prim, sitting up straight and smoothing out her skirt, "I found some tiny red maple leaves and Johnny-jump-ups to press in the dictionary."

"How nice. All right, now, let's everyone sit down and we'll have supper," said Gertrude. She and Omeletta bustled about with blooming cheeks and fresh pinafores, serving bowls of hot lentil soup and recounting their harrowing adventure.

"Let us say grace for this exciting day," said Arnold, beaming at his family gathered around the kitchen table, "and thank the Lord for all the good gifts we never expected, narrow escapes, nourishing food, a snug house, hot water, curly hair, books, the humans for having a pantry, chicken soup when you're sick, violins—"

"Let's *eat*," groaned Chester. And so they did.

Gertrude sipped her soup with an oyster cracker floating in the middle of the bowl. The only thing needed to make this blissful moment perfect, she thought, was a dollop of whipped cream for the tarts.

·4·

Chester's Rare Affliction

hester was in a snit. He sulked and pouted and was grumpy as a porcupine ready to shoot its quills. And it was all because of his mother.

Something had happened to her this morning. She had changed from his loving, understanding mother to a frowning, frumpy meanie. She said no to everything he wanted to do—take, for instance, going Downstairs by himself.

Chester longed to see the world beyond the boxes and old toys of the attic, beyond his family's reach and call. He had explored almost every nook and cranny of the attic, and was bored, *bored*, BORED.

Did his mother care? All she could say was "No, you can't go Downstairs alone. You can't go anywhere beyond the attic alone. It's much too dangerous."

He would have to wait until the family went to the country to visit Uncle Nathaniel, who would teach him the ways of eluding enemies. Chester didn't want to wait for a family trip. He didn't want to visit Uncle Nathaniel, who told long boring stories about his life as a detective and who never invited them to stay for dinner. Chester didn't even want to leave the house. All he wanted to do was go Downstairs. *By himself.* Why couldn't they understand?

It was such a simple request. He knew he was a smart, quick, agile mouse who could elude any danger. He must make his mother see this.

"Mother, please let me go Downstairs."

"Not today, Chester," said his mother.

"I don't see why not. It isn't fair. Omeletta got to go, and she's younger than me."

"That's right, and she almost drowned in a bowl of cream."

His pleading wore on
her like the drops of rain
hammering on the attic
roof and leaking through
onto the farmhouse.

The Band-Aid Arnold had patched on the roof had curled
up and dropped off.
They were out of candles
and poppy seeds and
peppermint tea, and there
was only enough cattail
flour left for a small batch

of scones. The girls had been
fighting all morning over
silly things. Now Prim had
an upset stomach from
eating too many cinnamon
red-hots, and Omeletta

had fallen from the rope
swing in the barn and
was seeing everything
double.

There was a bushel of beets to pickle, and the first yellow apples to make into sauce, and elderberries to dry for winter. To top it off, Arnold was away for three days at a librarians' convention. Gertrude had sent him off with his carpetbag filled with clean socks and underwear, an umbrella, his favorite Rum Maple tobacco, and a blue-silk smoking jacket for evening sessions.

She didn't begrudge his time away, but right this moment she gladly would have changed places with him. As much as she loved her children, they seemed quite obnoxious today and grated on her nerves. It was Chester's whining especially that drove her to desperate measures.

"Why can't I go Downstairs?" he repeated. "Why are you being so mean? I'm old enough. I'm smart. I won't get caught. Why won't you let me, Mother, *why?* I'll watch out for Max. Please, Mother, *please,* please let me, Daddy would let me go if he was here. I'll never bother you again if you'll just let me go this once, please, *please . . .*"

"I SAID NO, AND NOT ANOTHER WORD!"

Chester stamped his foot and clenched his fists, and before he could stop himself, the terrible, forbidden words in his mind were on his lips.

Chester had crossed the line. He had talked back.

Gertrude grabbed Chester by the ear and snapped, "That does it, young man. Talk back, will you? Argue with your mother? To think it has come to this, that I would ever see the day! When will you learn that when I say something, I mean it!"

She dragged Chester, squirming and crying and dragging his heels, into the bathroom and washed out his mouth with a sliver of red soap that smelled like a hospital and tasted like nasty medicine. Chester had never tasted anything so terrible in his life. He howled and gagged and snorted, and he knew

that he had the meanest, awfulest mother in the world, and he would never, ever forgive her.

He wriggled with all his might to break loose, which he finally did, leaving his mother holding his empty jacket.

"Chester! Chester, you come back here this very instant!" she yelled at her disappearing son. But Chester had already vanished from the farmhouse, out into the attic world that he found so boring.

"Very well, young man," said his mother, folding her arms. "Just wait until you come back. Just wait until your father gets home!" There was no point in going to look for him and wasting her afternoon. She had too much to do. She called the girls, and they set to work chopping beets and apples.

Chester had run blindly and jumped into the cup of the Christmas tree holder. His heart was pounding with panic and guilt. Never before had he defied his mother and run away. He waited cautiously for some time, until he was sure no one was coming after him. He heard no shrieking or yelling, so he supposed it was safe to stick his head up and check out the situation.

There, he thought cockily. I'm safe. I did what *I* wanted to do and got away with it. Chester would not admit to himself that now that he had the chance, he was afraid of going Downstairs alone. He told himself that he would rather hide out in the attic and have an afternoon of fun. To tell the truth, he was also afraid of being alone in the dark, among bats and spiders who came out at night, and he knew that when twilight came, he would have to go home to whatever awaited him. But he wasn't going to think about that now.

He ran lightly over the faces of old dolls, tweaked a teddy bear's nose, sat in the toy school-bus and pretended he was the driver, jumped on the strings of a tennis racket as if it were a trampoline, chewed a tiny hole in a pillow and watched the feathers float up like the down from milkweed pods. He nibbled on a few leaves of chamomile daisies drying for tea and thought what a glorious afternoon it was after all!

Then he spied a small white box tied with pink ribbon.

"Hello, what's this? What have we here?" he said seriously, pretending to be a detective. He put a sprig of chamomile in his mouth and puffed on it as if it were a pipe. "I've never seen that box before. I don't see why I have to wait until Sunday to see what's in it. There's no time like now. Righto!"

He quickly chewed through the ribbon and burrowed under the loose cover. A delicious, fruity perfume almost made him swoon. He sniffed deeply—raspberry! He could not get enough of the sweet fragrance of his favorite wild berry, and he remembered picnics in the woods in summer and tin buckets filled with berries for pie and jam. And now that unforgettable sweetness was right here in his attic.

The smell was so tantalizing, he began to nibble very gently around the edges of a small, round pink cake, around and around, until it looked like a pie with its crust pressed down with a fork. He could not stop. He had not eaten lunch, so his empty stomach was eager to be filled. Soon it was as round and full and pink as the little cake. He could barely crawl out of the box. Why, he wondered, would the humans put such a delicacy up in the attic?

Chester, despite his excellent opinion of himself, was very young, and he knew nothing about pretty cakes of soap that smelled like raspberries. He began to feel a bit dizzy and not sure of where his feet were going. He traveled very slowly along the shortest way home. His stomach, growing larger, dragged along the floor. Finally he reached the farmhouse and saw his mother through the kitchen window. Fear added to his dizziness. He could not bear the thought of a spanking the way he felt now!

His mother was waiting for him, but not as he expected. After she had washed out his mouth with soap, she had been filled with remorse. She wished she hadn't been so angry. Where had that child gone? He could have fallen headfirst into a box, in the mood he was in. Oh, if only Arnold were here!

When she saw Chester dragging slowly up the path, she ran to greet him. Her relief turned to concern when she saw his white face and his stomach tight as a pink puffball.

"Oh, my dear, what has happened? What's wrong?"

Chester was too sick to speak. He groaned and fell in a small gray heap at her feet. "Oh dear!" Gertrude wrung her hands and ran around and around in a circle. "What shall I do? Girls, come here this minute. Something has happened to Chester!"

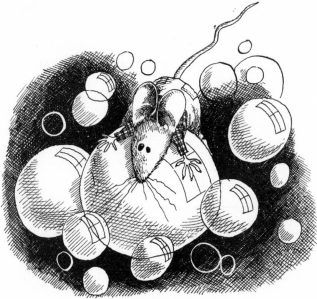

Prim and Omeletta came and watched Chester groan and writhe, his stomach growing larger by the moment.

"I must remain calm," said Gertrude, clasping her hands together tightly. "We must get the doctor. Prim, you can find the way to Dr. Mossberry's home. Go quickly, under the eaves, down the drainpipe, across the herb garden, down the gully, into the cellar of the grey stone house. There's a sign on his door—Dr. Augustus Mossberry. Tell him Chester's ill and to come quickly."

"Yes, ma'am," said Prim, excited by the chance to go Outside.

Gertrude and Omeletta carried Chester to his bed and dropped him in the center. Gertrude covered him with a quilt and put a hot-water bottle at his feet. She went into the kitchen and brought back some freshly squeezed lemonade in his favorite glass. "Here, dear, drink this," she said. "Lemon juice is good for everything."

Chester raised his head and managed a few gulps. Then he hiccuped. From his mouth came a large, perfectly shaped yellow bubble, followed by a trail

of small yellow bubbles. He hiccuped again, and again, and with each came more golden bubbles, until the room was afloat with them.

"My word," said his mother softly.

"Holy cow," whispered Omeletta. She reached over and gently pushed on Chester's stomach. A small cluster of bubbles escaped his mouth and rose to the ceiling.

Then they heard a rustling under the eaves and muffled talk, and Prim and Dr. Mossberry came hurrying up the path. Bubbles were bouncing around the farmyard and escaping from the chimney.

"Well, well, Chester," boomed the doctor, "what's going on here?" Dr. Mossberry was a forbidding figure, with a thick, pointed grey beard, a satin waistcoat that held his gold pocket watch, and bristly eyebrows that hung over his eyes like awnings. All the mice children were quiet and polite in his presence.

He held Chester's wrist and counted his pulse. "Hmmm," he said, frowning. He examined Chester's ears and eyes and nose and tail. He pressed his stomach, and more bubbles came out of Chester's mouth. Dr. Mossberry stroked his beard as he watched the bubbles rise to the ceiling.

"Hmmm," he said again. "A most interesting case. Gertrude," (he called Chester's mother Gertrude because he had known her since she was a little girl) "I'd like to try something. Would you have a glass of cranberry juice? I would like Chester to drink some."

"Oh, yes," said Gertrude, and she scurried into the kitchen and came out with a glass. "Freshly squeezed," she said with a touch of pride. "All our juice is freshly squeezed."

"Good. Now drink this, Chester. Slowly—"

Chester drank it down and promptly hiccuped. From his mouth there came again a perfect bubble, this one crimson, followed by bunches of small scarlet bubbles.

"Now, Chester, tell me the truth," said Dr. Mossberry. "Have you been getting into the wine in the pantry Downstairs?"

"Oh," gasped Gertrude, "surely not that!"

Chester shook his head no. He tried to talk, but only more hiccups and bubbles came out. The room looked quite beautiful as the afternoon sun cast a glow on the dancing bubbles.

Dr. Mossberry seemed not to notice the bubbles. He was unsmiling and serious. "Gertrude, would you have any grape juice?"

Gertrude rushed into the kitchen and brought out a glass of grape juice. "Freshly—"

"Yes, Gertrude, I know," said Dr. Mossberry. As soon as Chester drank it, he began to hiccup luscious purple bubbles, which mingled with the others on the ceiling.

Next Dr. Mossberry called for lime juice, and this time Chester hiccuped green bubbles as bright as the first grass of spring. Altogether the room was a rainbow of colored bubbles, each bumping into the other, all smelling strangely of raspberry.

Dr. Mossberry put his gold watch back into his pocket and stood up. He put his hands behind his back and began to pace back and forth. He looked long at Chester, a bit sadly, the boy thought.

"Chester, I fear you may have the rare affliction called bubblephilia. It is very rare—so rare, you may well be the only known case ever in the village. I shall have to watch you very closely, and you must obey my instructions to the minute or you may never again speak in the mouse tongue. You may have to go away to a school in the city, where you will learn to converse with others of your own kind."

"His own kind?" gasped Gertrude, her eyes filled with tears.

"Yes," said Dr. Mossberry solemnly. "Bubblephiliacs. But don't despair yet. It's possible, just possible, that Chester does not have this rare affliction. Miracles do happen, you know. Gertrude, may I speak with you in private?"

"Of course," sniffed Gertrude, wiping away her tears with her apron. To think of her dear little Chester, a bubblephiliac!

"Tell me, my dear," said the doctor kindly. "Has Chester ever shown a fondness for soap? Has he ever, to your knowledge, eaten it? Some children find it hard to resist, you know."

"Oh, no!" wailed Gertrude, and threw her head into her hands. "It's all my fault. I shouldn't have done it. I washed Chester's mouth out with Lifebouy because he was sassing me, and he must have swallowed some. Oh, to think my anger has caused him to have bubblephilia. . . . Will he ever forgive me?"

"Now, now," said Dr. Mossberry, still patting her on the shoulder. "It's really not as serious as I made it out to be. At least now we know what caused it. And you did what you thought was right. I know children can be a source of great annoyance. After all, I raised twelve myself." He laughed. "Chester will be himself in a few days. Uncomfortable, but good as new. My," he shook his head, "he certainly must have swallowed a goodly amount."

"I didn't think so," said Gertrude. "It was such awful-smelling stuff. It certainly didn't smell like raspberries."

"Well, all's well that ends well, my dear. I'll give you some licorice and wintergreen pills for him one every three hours, and you can start him on soft-boiled eggs and pea soup tomorrow. Now go back and assure Chester that you still love him," and he laughed his kindly, deep old-doctor laugh.

Chester, as he lay counting the bubbles on the ceiling, was in a state of quiet amazement at all that was happening—his adventure with the white box tied in pink ribbon, known only to him; these bubbles of many colors; his sisters treating him as if he were a person of importance; his mother crying over him, wanting to know if he'd like some fresh hot applesauce, as if he had never defied her.

He didn't understand why she wasn't still angry with him, but he was a smart mouse. He knew enough not to question it, nor had he any intention of telling any of them about the cake of raspberry soap.

Omeletta jumped up and down on his bed. "Come on, Chester, hiccup some more so we can see what color bubbles'll come out."

Chester knew that in a few days things would be back to normal. His mother would get angry with him again and his sisters would ignore him, but for now he could enjoy being the victim of a rare affliction.

"I'll try," he moaned softly.

·5·

A Private Place for Prim

erhaps it was approaching spring that made Prim restless and impatient with things as they were. Perhaps she was tired of being called Prissy Prim and being the caretaker of a sister who could have been from another planet. Perhaps she was tired of sleeping on graham-cracker crumbs, and finding orange pits in her books and her toothbrush wet.

Whatever the reason, Prim marched down to the kitchen one blustery morning in a mood as angry as the weather. She stood in front of Gertrude, her arms folded, eyebrows frowning. "Mother, I can't stand it any longer. I cannot live with that pig—"

"If you mean your sister, Omeletta, kindly call

her by name. There are no pigs living here. Furthermore, we do not use that kind of language. You may have a sister who is inclined to be sloppy and careless of the needs of others—"

"Inclined?" said Prim, exasperated. "I'd like to see anyone share a room with her and not get mad."

"Angry," corrected her mother.

"Angry, then. She makes me *very* angry. How can I ever become an artist if I can't even spread out my canvases and brushes and paints because my sister jumps into the paints and runs around the canvases making footprints? If she isn't a pig, then she's a slob."

Gertrude said nothing and kept snipping dandelions for the salad.

"Mother," said Prim, "I want a place of my own."

"Now you know we have only three bedrooms, dear. If Omeletta had been born a boy, you'd have your own room, but we can't change things, can we? Perhaps your father could fix up a nook in the hayloft. Would that do?"

"No, that's too close to home. I mean I want a place of my own *away* from home, far enough so I won't see or hear anyone. Just my own little refuge. I won't live there. I'll be home for supper. I just want a place to go when Omeletta and Chester become unbearable. I want to be able to be alone with my thoughts. You do understand, don't you?"

"Of course I do," said Gertrude. She knew it wasn't easy being an artist and living in the real world at the same time. "I'll speak to your father, and we'll see what we can do."

Arnold, having lived the life of a scholar, understood Prim's need even more than Gertrude. One needed a place just to *be*, a place to stand at the window and think without somebody asking what one was doing. Sometimes it took years of standing at the window before a great painting or poem or piece of music was created. Yes, Prim should have her place.

The next Sunday afternoon was spent apartment hunting. The mice didn't know exactly what they were looking for, but Prim said she would know it when she saw it. In the end it was Chester, who had gone off on his own, who found it.

He had scampered up the wall and seen it, the ice skate hanging by its shoelace from a nail. It wasn't very stylish—all black, with brown toe and tongue—but Chester could see it had possibilities. "Prim," he called from inside the toe, "come look at this. There's loads of room!"

Prim and the others hurried up the wall and examined every inch of the ice skate. "Good heavens," said Gertrude. "I knew humans had big feet, but this is incredible. It must fit a giant."

"I've found that young boy humans do tend to have big feet. It's nothing unusual," Arnold assured her.

Prim found it all wonderful and marvelous. "There's so much room—and I can get up and run a few laps when I'm tired of standing. And I like the way the sun shines in through the eyelets, and I can roll back the tongue for even more light. . . . Oh, isn't it wonderful, isn't it marvelous!"

That evening everyone carried something from home to help Prim set up her studio. Gertrude wiped away a small tear, to think her little girl was grown up enough to have her own place. Omeletta was happier than anyone, because now she would no longer be scolded as much for sleeping in her socks or throwing apple cores under the bed.

And so Prim painted away the spring and summer and fall, uninterrupted and undisturbed. By October, Prim had finished her major work, a portrait

of her parents for their anniversary. In it Arnold sat on the piano stool, his pipe in hand, with Gertrude standing by his side, her dainty hand gently draped over his shoulder. Her parents agreed that the painting was a masterpiece and hung it over the love seat in the parlor.

Prim's mind was simmering with other projects for the winter—a mosaic of beach glass, dried-flower pictures, acorn dolls. She had come in from the meadow with her arms full of pearly everlasting and grapevines for wreaths when she found her father waiting for her. His eyes were sad.

"Primrose, my dear," he began. She knew it must be serious if he called her Primrose.

"Primrose, I have unhappy news."

"Unhappy news?"

"Your studio is gone."

"Gone?" Prim dropped the vines and flowers. "Oh, no, I don't believe that. . . ."

She ran as fast as she could, scaling the boxes of wineglasses and good china to reach her refuge. It *was* gone. Only the nail remained.

"What happened?" She began to sob softly.

"The mistress came and took all the mittens and scarves and boots—and the skate. I don't know why she took one skate, but she did."

Prim wiped her eyes and nose and then sat very still, shivering now and then. She did not like to cry in front of anyone. She was not like Omeletta, who threw tantrums, or Chester, who whined. When she was upset, she said nothing, went to her room, threw herself across her bed, and cried until the tears soaked through the featherbed comforter.

"All my paints, my brushes, my easel, the smock Aunt Lucy made from her red nightie—everything's gone. I wonder what the humans will say when they find them."

"Well, if I know humans, they probably didn't even see them," Arnold consoled her. "The mistress probably just shook the skate over the trash can, trying to get out any dead spiders, and didn't even look. Maybe she just threw the skate out. Humans can be insensitive."

By now Gertrude and Omeletta and Chester had

learned about the disaster and came to comfort Prim, taking turns with hugs and murmurings.

"Dumb old humans," said Chester, "always messing things up."

"Well, it *is* their skate," said Gertrude, determined to be fair. "I just never thought they would have a use for it. But you never can tell with humans, can you?"

Arnold, trying to lighten the gloom, told Prim to count her blessings. First of all she could have been *in* the skate when it was whisked off.

"And that would have been a real tragedy. This is just a minor setback. All artists must suffer setbacks, but the great ones *persevere*. Did you know

that Leonardo da Vinci
painted *The Last Supper* on
damp walls, and first thing
you know, the paint began
to slip and slide, and why,
it was so bad, even the

bread in our Lord's hand grew mold!''

Prim stopped sniffling and thought
about this. Arnold, happy
to divert her, went on to
tell stories of painters
who went blind, musicians who
became deaf, dancers who got frostbite, chefs who
lost their taste—all of whom
rose to greater fame
because they *persevered*.

"Okay, so let's go find
another place," said
Omeletta, who couldn't
sit still very long. "Someplace no one is ever going
to need or take or move." She had enjoyed Prim's
being away and wanted to keep it that way.

Again the family went on an expedition to find a place for Prim. One after the other, possibilities were looked at and rejected because of flaws. A blue enamel teakettle, spacious yet cozy, was coated with rust on the inside, and Arnold feared Prim might breathe it into her lungs. A pink-glass globe for an oil lamp delighted Prim, but Gertrude shook her head no. Too fragile, too dangerous. A square red-plaid tin that had once held shortbread was clean and pleasant but not deep enough. Prim couldn't set up her easel without hitting her head. A wicker basket that was roomy and airy, and filtered the light in just right, seemed perfect. But Prim, fearing the humans might come and take it, would not consider it.

Chester, whose enthusiasm was waning, said, "Well, what *do* you want? Nothing pleases you. There's something wrong with everything we find."

Prim sighed. Nobody understood. She wanted to cry, but wouldn't in front of the others.

"I'm sorry I'm such a bother," she said in a small, stiff voice. "I think I'll just go off by myself, if you don't mind." Before they could stop her, she disappeared under the eaves.

When she could no longer hold back the tears, she slumped down onto the floor and let them flow. The late-afternoon sun came through the attic window in golden streams. Even the specks of dust dancing in it were golden. She loved this time of day, when everything was bathed in an otherworldly

gold. Oh, to have a studio filled with that light, with windows framing the world outside, making her a part of it, yet secure within! Oh, her heart ached with yearning and a small, growing despair. Was it too much to ask for a refuge where she might paint or press flowers or yodel or dance a schottische or do anything she wanted?

She put up with so much, asked so little, suffered the scorn of the misunderstood artist with such undying grace—was she not entitled to some crumbs of happiness? Why had she been born into such an unimaginative (albeit well-meaning), normal—she shuddered at the word—family, when her soul was to the manor born, a manor with solarium studio just for her?

She sighed deeply. Self-pity oozed and threatened to overflow into tears again. But sad as she was, she would not let this happen. She knew the true artist should not, could not, be bound by circumstance. She would overcome; she would find truth and beauty in whatever life gave her and capture it on canvas. Someday, when her gift was recognized, and stories were written about her in magazines about how she had overcome her deprived childhood, her family would understand and be sorry. She would forgive them graciously, even that slobby Omeletta.

Cheered by the thought of humbling her sister, Prim almost smiled. She dried her eyes with her petticoat and leaned back for a good stretch before rejoining the others. She felt something cold and hard at her back. She hadn't noticed it before, but it had been darker then, and she'd been distraught.

She felt her way cautiously around the object, which seemed to be a rectangle. The afternoon sun Prim so admired had made its way in fingerlike streaks across the attic and into the eaves, and Prim

now saw what she had been leaning against as she was pouring out her woes.

She called to the others to come quickly and see what she had found. They rallied to the excitement in Prim's voice and gathered around her discovery. Little streams of sun shone like spotlights on it. For once, they were all speechless.

"My word," said Arnold finally. "It's an old aquarium!"

They moved slowly, single file, around it. The walls of thick green glass were so dirty, they could barely see through them. Inside were all manner of mysterious things—a castle with turrets and archway, a china sea-horse, a statue of Pan playing his pipes. The floor was covered with small white pebbles and periwinkle shells. Over everything hung dust and cobwebs.

"This looks like something out of *Great Expectations*!" whispered Arnold.

Chester, who had already climbed in, scooped up some pebbles and put them in his pocket. He liked the feel of them.

Gertrude wondered why they had never found this place before. It must have been here for years, judging from the dust. How could they have overlooked it on their Sunday jaunts?

Arnold, reading her mind, chuckled and said, "Well, you know what they say. Sometimes you can't see the forest for the trees. Or—is it, you can't see the trees for the forest?"

Gertrude just smiled and nodded. Either way, it didn't make much sense to her. The important thing was that they had found it, and with a bit of work Prim would now have her place. Gertrude thought what a lovely place this would have been for the Ladies' Sewing Circle meetings, once the statue of Pan was removed.

Aloud she said, "Before we do anything else, we've got to get rid of this dirt. What good is a glass house if you can't see through it?"

And so they set to work, armed with mops and polishing cloths and brooms and jugs of vinegar and water. Before sunset the next day, they had changed the old fish tank into Prim's light-filled studio. They felt achy and cranky and pleased and proud, which, as Arnold said, was the proper way to feel after a good day's work.

Even Omeletta wished she had a place like this and said so. Prim wondered how it would look after one day with Omeletta.

"You know, Prim," said her sister, "you really ought to thank me for being so sloppy. If I were neat and prissy like you, you'd never have found such a place!"

"I suppose you're right," said Prim, and hugged her little sister carefully (Omeletta had been eating chocolate). If Omeletta followed Prim's example, there was yet hope she might grow up to be a lovable, even respectable, mouse.

"There's just one small thing that bothers me," said Prim.

"And that is?" asked her parents.

"It's a lovely place, but— I feel as if I'm living in a goldfish bowl."

"My dear," said Arnold, "it *is* a goldfish bowl. Be thankful the goldfish left and *persevere*."

And so she did.

·6·

The Attic Crèche

t was the week before Christmas, and the attic mice threw themselves into a flurry of busyness for the celebration. They scrubbed and swept and polished silver and baked pastries and steamed puddings and wrapped secret presents and loved every minute of it. Omeletta flopped down after taking a tray of gingerbread cats out of the oven and sighed, "I'm so happy, I just can't stand it!"

"You took the words right out of my mouth," said Gertrude, whose hands and face seemed always dusted with flour these days. Her mind was working as busily as her hands to think up a new way to show their happiness, something beyond cleaning and feasting and trimming the tree. What they needed was a tradition, a special Christmas tradition that would become a sweet memory as the years passed.

She and Arnold had such memories, lovingly brought out and shared with the children each Christmas. Arnold told how he and the other members of the Bachelors' Club at the University would go caroling, and come back to the library and hot mugs of rum and imported cigars and good conversation. "Such a fellowship we had," he sighed, remembering.

Gertrude had been in charge of the church-mice choir before she met Arnold. How sweet it had been, she told them, to lead the choir on Christmas Eve in their carols at the manger after Midnight Mass! They had the Christ Child all to themselves as they sat on the splintery edges of the manger and sang their little mouse hearts out in the shadowy light of the candles.

And as a special gift, they would arrange a Living Tableau for the Child. Gertrude had a talent for such presentations (the mice elders had once awarded her a plaque for Unique Artistic Achievement). She would choose an important moment in the Old Testament and portray it with the mouse choir as if it were a painting.

When all was at the moment of perfection, she would whisper, "Freeze!" From that instant until she snapped her fingers releasing them, no whisker or tail twitched, no nerve rippled or nose sneezed. They were frozen as statues. Oh, now and then a

minor disaster occurred, such as in the homecoming scene of "The Prodigal Son." The little fellow who was the Fatted Calf took a fit of giggling and fell off the spit. But the audience laughed in good humor,

for he was a very young mouse and it was his first
Tableau. Gertrude took five curtain calls that night
and had to grant an encore, for which she was pre-
pared ("Moses Parting the Red Sea").

Ah, those were the days, sighed Gertrude. But
she was not one to sigh and let it go at that. Someday *this* Christmas would be the old days to the
children. Now was the time to start a tradition.
Their own crèche must be a good one, for what is
Christmas without honoring the Child? Perhaps they
might build one outdoors in the farmyard next to
the silo? But how? Arnold was a literary mouse with
no talent for carpentry, and Chester was the image
of his father.

Could she and the girls do it? No, that would
hurt Arnold's and Chester's feelings, and besides, the
girls could do nothing together without fighting. She
waited for inspiration.

On Sunday, as usual, they went on their expedition to discover the contents of boxes brought up
during the week. There was nothing of interest today except a box of old *Countryman* magazines, to

which Arnold would return when he was alone. He had noticed, in a quick skimming of the top one, an article on walking sticks that might prove interesting.

Then Omeletta, who had gone exploring on her own, squealed from a far corner under the eaves, "I found something! Wait a minute— I think—" She scratched and sniffed and coughed from the dust and finally yelled, "Hurrah! Guess what I found—I think it's a crèche! Hurry, come see!"

The mice scrambled to the corner and joined Omeletta. They pulled and tugged at the box until they tipped it over and spilled its contents onto the floor. Not only was it indeed a crèche, with thatched roof and an empty manger the size of a matchbox, it was also filled with toy animals of all description.

With excitement the mice uncovered the objects wrapped in brittle newspaper blankets. "Look at this, Gertrude," said Arnold. "The date on this paper is January 16, 1932! Why, this crèche must have belonged to the grandmother of the house—"

"Oh, look," whispered Prim as she held a blue-glass bird up to catch the light of the afternoon sun.

"And look at this." Omeletta laughed as she lifted a small, white wooden rabbit with green waistcoat and drum.

"And this!" Chester shook a saltshaker in the shape of a turkey with holes in his tail.

"What a strange gathering," mused Arnold. "One would expect to find the normal amount of cows and sheep, but these are quite unusual, I must say."

"There's more," said Chester, and he dove pell-mell into the newspapers at the bottom of the box. Up he came, as if surfacing from under waves, with several larger animals, which with some grunting and heaving the others helped carry away.

The mouse family lined the animals up on the floor and examined them. There was a blue pottery pony from Mexico with white flowing mane and poppies painted on his saddle. A yellow china pig. A fuzzy red reindeer with one gold antler. A black china pie-bird, his beak lifted in song. Three monkeys joined together, their paws covering their eyes, ears, and mouth. There was even a cream-colored calico cat, lying with her paws tucked beneath her.

Omeletta was all for leaving the cat in the box, but Gertrude, ever mindful of giving good example, would not allow it. "It is Christmas, and we must try to love everyone. Even a cat." At least we can try, she thought.

So they set about moving the crèche to the barn-yard. Prim got her red wagon and Chester the wheelbarrow, and slowly, with everyone steadying it, they wheeled the crèche across the attic and into its spot by the silo. They were quite amazed at what they had done. Then Chester said matter-of-factly, "You know, there's no Baby Jesus. No Holy Family. No Wise Men, either."

The mice fell silent. "Whatever could have happened to them?" said Gertrude. "What good is a crèche without the main characters?"

Arnold pulled on his pipe thoughtfully. His eyes met the eyes of his wife, who at that very moment had what she knew to be a Divine Inspiration. His eyes began to twinkle. Being a husband and wife in love, they often could read each other's minds.

"My dear," he said, "I think it's time for you to create one of your famous Living Tableaux. Think about it—what do we have here? Five mice—five exceptionally talented mice, I might add. Mice who never say no to a challenge, am I right?"

Gertrude, flushed and happy, agreed. "A marvelous suggestion! What do you say, children? Are you game? Of course, it's been so long since I directed— well, we're doing it for the Christ Child, and surely He won't be too critical. Now," she said, her mind already spinning plans, "your father will be Joseph, and I will be Mary, and you three will be the Wise Men. Aren't we lucky to have just the right number?"

"We have no Baby Jesus," said Prim.

"Hmmm," said Gertrude thoughtfully. "You're right. We need a Baby Jesus. Now, where shall we find Him? What can we use?"

"How about my Baby Mousekins doll?" said Prim. "She's just the right size—"

"No!" interrupted Omeletta. She thought Baby Mousekins was the dumbest doll she'd ever seen, and ugly too. "I've got something better." She looked around wildly, and her eyes fell on the wreath on the farmhouse door. "The chestnut! He'd be perfect!"

They all agreed, even Prim, reluctantly, that yes, he would be perfect. And so they began rehearsing that very evening after supper.

For the rest of the week, they pinned and clipped, scissored and sewed. They even made forays into the sewing room and kitchen Downstairs for odds and ends of satin and cork and lace and crayon. They found a piece of green flannel with candy canes on it, just the right size for a swaddling blanket for the Baby Jesus.

They rehearsed their carols in harmony. Arnold sang bass; Chester, tenor; the girls, wavery soprano; and Gertrude, a deep, mellow alto. In the evenings, when the dishes were done, they gathered in the living room and strung partridgeberries for the tree, singing "It Came Upon the Midnight Clear," and wondered impatiently if that midnight clear would ever come.

Finally it arrived. The moon shone full and bright, and a few snowflakes danced outside the attic window. The farmhouse sparkled with cleanliness and twinkling tree-lights, and the air hung with the fragrance of pine needles strewn on the floor of the crèche. The toy animals circled the empty manger bedded with a thimbleful of straw. At the stroke of midnight from the grandfather clock Downstairs, the solemn, reverent procession of mice began. As they walked, they sang "We Three Kings of Orient Are."

First came Joseph in a striped robe (cut from a kitchen towel), leading the way with a candy-cane staff. Gertrude followed, eyes lowered, her face

framed in a blue-satin mantle embroidered with pink
stars. She held the Baby Jesus chestnut tightly in her
arms. Next came the Wise Men in order of age:
Prim, in a blue-lace robe (made from an old curtain)
and silver-thimble crown; Chester, trying not to
tread on the hem of his purple-silk robe (cut from
a necktie) or to trip on the chain of paper clips
hanging from his waist; Omeletta, in a tunic of gold
sequins and fringes (part of a lady's evening bag),
beating her tambourine and dancing in her bare feet
to the music.

The Wise Men had begun to offer their gifts—
three grains of barley, a patchwork pillow, a
chocolate-covered raisin—when Gertrude's sensitive

ears caught the sound of danger, a soft, padding sound. Terror fluttered her heart as she saw Max the cat coming slowly up the stairs. Fat, mean Max, who was to be feared as much as the humans, even though his eyes were losing their sharpness.

What was he doing here? Had he planned to do them in on this sacred night? Gertrude could not know that Max, tired of the holiday noise and teasing of visitors, had come to the attic to get away from it all and sleep.

When he reached the top of the stairs, he collapsed in a furry, rumpled pile. Before he shut his

rheumy eyes, he thought he saw two mice standing over a manger, two other mice offering gifts to a chestnut in the manger, and another, slightly wild mouse dancing and beating a tambourine. His eyes widened and his mouth opened and his tail grew thick and started to quiver.

At that moment Gertrude whispered the word "Freeze!" and the mice turned as lifeless as the toy animals. Joseph patted the Mexican pony, Mary cuddled the Child, Chester held out his gift of three grains of barley. Prim curtseyed, and Omeletta stretched her leg in an arabesque and raised the tambourine high above her head.

Not a whisker twitched, not a breath heaved their chests. The old cat blinked several times and began to drool, which embarrassed him. Mice in a crèche? One wearing a thimble, another shaking a tambourine? He decided his mind was wandering. He would go back Downstairs and find a safe, quiet place under a bed. He preferred noise to bewitchment. As softly as he had come up the stairs, he went back down, at a faster pace.

The mice were jubilant! To get the better of mighty Max was no mean feat. They hugged and kissed and wished each other Merry Christmas and sang "The Holly and the Ivy" all the way back to the farmhouse, where they sat down to the table spread with persimmon pudding and sugared almond-cakes and freshly squeezed cider.

After the children, stuffed and sleepy, finally went to bed, Gertrude and Arnold sat together in the love seat and watched the tree lights blink.

"Tonight was a masterpiece, my dear," said Arnold.

"Oh, I'd say more of a small triumph," said Gertrude modestly.

"And the beginning of a tradition," added her husband.

"Yes, indeed," smiled Gertrude, her mind already busy with plans for the second annual production of *The Attic Players' Christmas Tableau.*

·7·

Epilogue

The years passed, and the mouse children, like all children, grew up and moved away.

Prim married an English professor and lived in a dollhouse mansion in Boston. It was everything her mother had ever wanted, even to the burnished gold faucets in the bathroom and the gazebo out back. They had one daughter, Chrysanthemum, who was fat and jolly and became a renowned pastry chef. Her cheesecakes won awards.

Prim did not become the renowned artist of her youthful dreams (although a Boston art critic once said her portrait of Chrysanthemum resembled a very good Felicia Fernbottom, who was a very good student of Mary Cassatt).

Omeletta married a local church mouse who became a minister. She organized bazaars, poured tea, and led the choir. They had four sons, Matthew,

Mark, Luke, and Lancelot, all of whom made names for themselves as hockey players. Lancelot eventually gave it up, moved to England, and became a successful Shakespearean actor. He gave all credit to his grandmother and her family theatricals.

Chester became a poet
and mushroom expert and
went to live in the woods
where life was simple. He
never married, and came
home on weekends.

Gertrude and Arnold remained in the attic farmhouse, happy with their memories and their pride
in their children. Little-Good-for-Nothing was kept
in the hayloft of the barn, where the grandchildren
could play with him when they visited.

He had shriveled with age, his shine had dulled, and his skin was no longer smooth as satin. Prim's painted flowers had faded and almost disappeared. But the family loved him still. He had been a part of their youth and now shared their old age.

Little-Good-for-Nothing marveled at the happenings of his life. He had not, after all, been good for nothing. He had been useful and given pleasure and comfort. He had touched a part of their lives.

True, it was only a small part, but then Little-Good-for-Nothing was a very small chestnut.